iVy + BEAN

BOOK 6

EVERYBODY LOVES IVY + BEAN!

"The deliciousness is in the details." — ★*Booklist*, starred review

"Ivy and Bean are irresistible." — ★*Kirkus Reviews*, starred review

"This story defies expectations of what an early chapter book can be."
—*School Library Journal*

". . . the series' strong suits are humor and the spot-on take on relationships."—*Booklist*

"Text and illustrations are as fine a match as Ivy and Bean."
—*The Horn Book*

iVy + BEAN
DOOMED TO DANCE

BOOK 6

written by annie barrows + illustrated by sophie blackall

chronicle books · san francisco

For Esme and Megan, friends from the beginning —A. B.

For the other Ivy, and her brother, Moss —S. B.

Thanks to Dr. George Matsumoto of the Monterey Bay
Aquarium Research Institute for useful information regarding squid.

Book design by Sara Gillingham.
Typeset in Blockhead and Candida.
The illustrations in this book were rendered in Chinese ink.

Library of Congress Cataloging-in-Publication Data
Barrows, Annie.
Ivy and Bean doomed to dance / written by Annie Barrows ; illustrated by Sophie Blackall.
p. cm. — (Ivy and Bean ; bk. 6)
Summary: Second-grade best friends Ivy and Bean beg for ballet lessons, then, when they
are cast as squids in their first recital, scheme to find a way out of what seems to be boring,
hard, and potentially embarrassing.
ISBN 978-0-8118-6266-0
[1. Ballet—Fiction. 2. Best friends—Fiction. 3. Friendship—Fiction.] I. Blackall, Sophie, ill.
II. Title. III. Title: Ivy and Bean doomed to dance. IV. Title: Doomed to dance.
PZ7.B27576Iwb 2009
[E]—dc22
2009004367

Manufactured by Friesens Corporation, Altona, Manitoba, Canada in December 2009.

10 9 8 7 6 5

This product conforms to CPSIA 2008.

Chronicle Books LLC
680 Second Street, San Francisco, California 94107

www.chroniclekids.com

CONTENTS

BALLET OR BUST

It was a book that started all the trouble. "Read, read, read! That's all grown-ups ever say to me," said Bean, "but when I finally do read, I get in trouble." She slumped in her chair. "And then the grown-ups take the book away."

Ivy nodded. "It's totally not fair," she agreed. "And they shouldn't blame us anyway. It's all Grandma's fault."

Ivy's grandma had sent her the book. It was called *The Royal Book of the Ballet*. Each chapter told the story of a different ballet, with pictures of fancy girls in feathery tutus and satin toe shoes.

Bean was at Ivy's house on the day it arrived. They were supposed to be subtracting, but they were tired of that so they ripped open the package and sat down side by side on Ivy's couch to look at *The Royal Book of the Ballet*.

"I heard that sometimes their toes bleed when they're dancing," said Bean. "The blood leaks right through the satin part."

"That's gross," said Ivy, turning the pages. Suddenly she stopped.

"Whoa, Nellie," murmured Bean, staring.

"Is she kicking his head off?" asked Ivy in a whisper.

"That's what it looks like," said Bean. "What's this one called, anyway?"

Ivy flipped back a few pages. "*Giselle*," she said, reading quickly. "It's about a girl named Giselle who, um, dances with this duke guy, but he's going to marry a princess, not Giselle, so she takes his sword and stabs herself." Ivy and Bean found the picture of that.

"Ew," said Bean. "But interesting."

"Yeah, and then she turns into a ghost with all these other girls. They're called the Wilis."

The picture showed a troop of beautiful women dressed in white. They had very long fingernails.

"And then," Ivy read on, "the duke goes to see Giselle's grave, and she comes out with the Wilis, and they decide to dance him to death." Ivy stared at the picture. "To *death*."

Bean leaned over for a closer look. It was pretty amazing. Giselle's pointed toe had snapped the duke's head up so that his chin pointed straight up to the sky. It would fall off in a moment. The Wilis stood in a circle, waving their long fingernails admiringly.

Bean lifted the page, wishing that she could see more of the picture, but there was no more. There never was. "Wow," she said, shaking her head. "She showed him."

For a few minutes, Ivy and Bean sat in silence, thinking.

"Okay," Ivy said finally. "I'm Giselle, and you're the duke."

"All right," said Bean. "But next time, I get to be Giselle."

It was fun playing Giselle, even though Ivy's mom wouldn't let them dance with a knife and they had to use a Wiffle bat instead. After they had each been Giselle a couple of times, they were Wilis, waving long Scotch-tape fingernails as they danced various people to death.

"Mrs. Noble!" shrieked Bean. "I'm dancing Mrs. Noble to death." Ivy ran to get a pair of her mother's high heels and pretended to be Mrs. Noble, a fifth-grade teacher who had once given Ivy and Bean a lot of trouble.

Bean the Wili chased Mrs. Noble around the house, waggling her fingernails and screaming. Finally, when they were both laughing so hard they couldn't dance any more, they rushed into the kitchen and fell over on the floor.

"Well, look who's here," said Ivy's mom. She was making dinner.

"Mom," Ivy said when she got her breath back, "I *have* to take ballet class."

Ivy's mom stirred something into something else. "You had to take ice-skating, too."

Ivy wiggled her toes. "Yeah, but that was a mistake."

"How do you know ballet isn't a mistake, too? Those skates were expensive."

"Ballet is different," Ivy explained. "Ballet isn't freezing and dumb. Ballet is pretty. And it's good for you."

"I'm going to take it, too," Bean said. "That way, we can help each other during the hard parts."

Ivy's mom looked at Bean in a surprised sort of way. "You're going to take ballet?"

"Sure." Bean's mom would be happy to let her take ballet. Bean was certain of it. After all, Bean thought, her mother liked nice stuff. And ballet was nice. Except for the part where you danced people to death.

+ + + + + +

The funny thing was, Bean's mother wasn't happy to let her take ballet. Not at all.

"You'll start it, and then you'll decide you hate it and want to quit."

"No, I won't. I'll love it," Bean said.

"I'll bet you a dollar you'll hate it," said Nancy. Nancy had taken ballet when she was Bean's age. Bean remembered the time Nancy had cried because she was a chocolate bar in a ballet about candy.

"But I'm not going to be a dorky old piece of candy," Bean said. "I'm going to be a Wili." She knew better than to tell Nancy that she was going to be Giselle. Nancy would just make fun of her.

"Ha," said Nancy. "You have to be whatever they tell you to be."

"Nancy," said her mom. "I'll discuss this with Bean in private, please."

"I'll bet you, Mom," said Nancy, getting up. "I'll bet you two dollars she quits after a week."

"I'll bet you a hundred I don't," said Bean.

"Good-bye, Nancy," said their mother.

Nancy left, and Mom turned to Bean. "Now, honey, I didn't want to go into this in front of Nancy, but if I do let you take ballet, there will be no quitting."

"Quitting? Why would I quit?"

"You quit softball."

"But that was softball. All you do in softball is stand around waiting for five hundred years until it's time to hit the stupid ball. And then you miss anyway. Ballet isn't like that."

Her mother looked at her.

Bean made her eyes big. "I thought you wanted me to learn new things," she said.

Her mother looked at her some more.

"Nancy got to take ballet." Bean wiggled her lower lip. She knew that a trembling lower lip is very sad looking.

Her mother laughed. "You're drooling. Okay. I will let you take ballet on one condition, and here it is: You will go for the whole session. Four months. Sixteen lessons One performance. No quitting. And no complaining."

"No problem!" said Bean. She jumped up and hugged her mother. "When can I start? I already know how to kick—you want to see?"

DIP, DIP, CRASH!

It was not long before Ivy and Bean realized that they had made a terrible mistake.

Bean began to realize it while Madame Joy was talking about first position. You stuck your heels together and your toes apart. Big deal. Where was the leaping? Where was the kicking? Where was the dancing?

Then Madame Joy chattered for a long time about nice round arms. Who cared about arms? When Madame Joy started in on second position, which turned out to be just regular standing, Bean stopped listening.

Ivy paid careful attention to first position. Heels, toes. Great! Then she paid careful attention to second position. Arms out, legs out. Great! Then came third position.

"Now," said Madame Joy, "third position. For third position, we slide our right foot, like so, to the middle of our left foot. Then we lift one nice round arm up, up in the air, leaving our other nice round arm—"

Ivy fell over with a thump.

"Goodness!" exclaimed Madame Joy. "Let's try that again."

Let's not, thought Ivy.

But they did. In fact, they did nothing but one, two, three, four, and five for half an hour. After that, Madame Joy showed them something called a plié. She acted like it was the most important

thing in the world, but really it was just bending your knees and dipping a little. Dip, dip,
dip. Row, row, row your boat, thought Bean.

"Hey, guys," she called, "Get this!" She
sang, "Dip, dip, dip your knees—"

Nobody joined in. Instead, Madame Joy said,
"We save our singing for after class, Bean."

Sheesh, Bean said to herself. You'd think she'd be happy to get a little more pep in here.

But it was even worse when Madame Joy was peppy. "All right, girls! Time to leap like little kitties!" Madame Joy said, springing into the air with her ballet slippers fluttering.

"She doesn't leap like a kitty. She leaps like a frog," Bean whispered to Ivy.

"Bean!" called Madame Joy. "You may lead the kitties." She twirled briskly around and hauled Bean to the front of the line. "Now," she said, smiling, "you are a kitty! Leap!" Madame Joy bounded across the wide, empty floor.

Bean closed her eyes and imagined she was a cat.

She was a skinny black cat that wanted to catch a bird. And then eat it. Bean crouched. She twitched her tail. She narrowed her eyes. "RRRRRrrrowll!" she screeched and then lunged forward, landing on her hands and knees in the middle of the floor. "Got him!" she yelled.

Madame Joy stared at Bean for a second, and then she said, "Dulcie, will you show us how to leap like a kitty?"

"Yes, Madame Joy," said Dulcie, only she said, "Madame Jwah." For some reason, Madame Joy liked that. Dulcie came to the front of the line and stood with her arms out and her toes pointed.

Bean rose to her feet. "So I already did it, right?" she asked. "I get to be done, right?"

"No," said Madame Joy. "You need more practice. Go to the end of the line."

Bean clomped to the end of the line and stood behind Ivy.

Dulcie lifted her arms higher and smiled proudly. Then she hopped across the empty floor, ker-plop, ker-plop. When she reached the other side of the ballet studio, Dulcie stood before Madame Joy and held out her tiny pink dance skirt. Then she swirled one leg behind the other and curtseyed.

"Show-off," whispered Bean.

"I can't believe that we asked for this," said Ivy, her eyes on Dulcie.

"We didn't just ask. We begged," Bean said glumly.

It was true. They had begged.

+ + + + + +

After everyone had leaped, Madame Joy clapped her hands and told them they had to be butterflies.

Bean raised her hand. "Can I be a Wili instead?"

Madame Joy stared at her. "Not today," she said in a way that really meant never. Then she turned on some music, and all the other girls ran around the room flapping their arms and pointing their toes.

That's when Ivy and Bean turned to look at each other, and their eyes said *We have made a terrible mistake.*

BAD NEWS
BENEATH THE SEA

Every week Bean and Ivy put on tights and leotards and went to Madame Joy's School of the Ballet, where they fell down and hurt themselves (Ivy) and were bored out of their minds (Bean). Every week they were told to watch Dulcie plié and kitty-jump across the floor even though she was only five. Every week they waited and waited for Madame Joy to clap her hands and say it was time to be butterflies. They hated being butterflies, but at least that meant ballet class was almost over.

It seemed like it couldn't get worse. And then one day, instead of telling them to be butterflies, Madame Joy told them to sit in a circle on the floor.

"We're going to be mushrooms," whispered Ivy to Bean.

Bean didn't think so. When grown-ups asked you to sit in a circle, they were usually about to tell you something you didn't want to hear. Ms. Aruba-Tate, Ivy and Bean's second-grade teacher, was forever gathering them in a circle for bad news. Like, the class fish died over the weekend. Or, everyone has to start using real punctuation. Or, the pencil sharpener is off-limits. Circles meant trouble.

Bean watched Madame Joy walk pointy-toed to a chair and sit. No floor for her. "Girls," she began, "I have something very special to tell you."

"Oh, tell us, Madame Jwah!" cried Dulcie. She even clapped her hands.

Madame Joy smiled. "As many of you know, we end each session with a lovely recital. A recital, girls, is a chance for you to dance before your friends and family so that they can see what you've learned."

Ivy coughed.

Madame Joy leaned forward eagerly. "Most of our recitals are held here at the school, but this time we have been invited to participate in The World of Dance! Isn't that wonderful?"

Several girls said, "*Oooooooh!*"

Bean was getting a not-so-good feeling. "What's The World of Dance?" she asked.

Madame Joy's smile grew. "The World of Dance is a gathering of many different dance schools from all over town—tap dancers, jazz dancers, hip-hop dancers. We will be representing the ballet. Each group gets a chance to perform, just as in a regular recital, but we'll be performing on a real stage in a real theater!"

"*Oooooooh!*" repeated the same girls.

Bean was sick of hearing that.

Ivy's hand shot into the air. "Can we do *Giselle?*"

"*Giselle?*" Madame Joy looked surprised. "No. Goodness, no. We will be doing a lovely piece called 'Wedding Beneath the Sea.'"

"Wedding Beneath the Sea"? Bean didn't care if she was rude. She yelled, "What are Ivy and me?"

Madame Joy raised her eyebrows. "I was planning to discuss parts next, but if you must know, you and Ivy will be the two friendly squids."

Nobody said, "Oooooooh." Squids? Ivy and Bean looked at each other. *We have made a really terrible mistake.*

On the drive home, Bean and Ivy were quiet. That was because of the no-complaining rule.

Quietly, they got out of the car and went into Bean's backyard. Quietly, they stuffed themselves into Bean's tiny playhouse and slumped against the walls.

"Squids. Who ever heard of squids?" said Bean. "I don't even know what squids are."

"I'm not totally sure," said Ivy, "but I think they're ugly, and I think people eat them."

"Oh, great," moaned Bean. "I can't believe that stupid Dulcie gets to be the mermaid, and we're squids."

"I believe it," said Ivy. "We're awful."

"We're not *awful*—" began Bean.

"Oh yes we are," said Ivy. "I'm worse than you, but you're pretty bad, too."

"That's because we hate it. If we liked it, we'd be better at it."

"I thought I'd like it," said Ivy sadly.

"So did I," said Bean. "I thought we'd be kicking some heads off. I didn't know about the positions and pliés and all that."

"You know, they can't *make* us do it," said Ivy.

Bean thought about that. "Yes, they can," she said.

Ivy sighed. "It was mean of them to make us promise not to complain," she said.

"Yeah," said Bean. "They knew all along how horrible it would be."

"We're going to have to be squids in front of everybody," said Ivy. "That's the most horrible thing of all."

"They'll probably laugh at us," said Bean, imagining it.

"They can't. They're *parents*," Ivy said.

"Remember? It's friends, too. There might even be someone from school there," Bean said gloomily.

"If only we could quit," Ivy moaned.

"But we can't," said Bean.

Ivy frowned. That meant she was getting determined. "There has to be a way," she said, determinedly. "Nothing is impossible."

Bean stared at her. "It's impossible for us to be good at ballet."

"Well, *that*, sure," said Ivy. "But it's not impossible for us to break our arms."

SQUIDS IN A FIX

"What?" said Bean.

"We can't be squids if we break our arms," said Ivy. "Remember what Madame Joy said? We're supposed to wave our tentacles gently on the passing tide. No way can we do that if we've got broken arms. Right?"

That was true. But. Broken arms. That could be going too far. Bean pictured her arm cracked in half.

"I saw a picture of a guy who broke his arm, and his bone poked out of his skin," she said.

Ivy made an ouch face.

"Yeah, I know," said Bean. "Maybe we don't have to break them. Maybe we can just sprain them instead." She didn't really know what a sprain was, but she knew that it didn't involve bones poking out of your skin.

"Okay. Sure. We can't be squids with sprained arms either," said Ivy. "No way."

"No how," agreed Bean. They looked at each other. "So, how do you sprain an arm?" Bean asked.

"I bet it's like breaking, only smaller," Ivy reasoned. "When she was a kid, my mom broke her arm falling off her garage roof. If we want to just sprain our arms, maybe we should find something shorter than a garage and fall off it."

42

This made sense. Bean looked around her backyard. There was the porch, but they'd crack their heads open on the stairs. There was the playhouse. There was the trampoline—"Hey, I've got an idea," Bean said. "We'll jump off the playhouse onto the trampoline and then boing from the trampoline onto the ground. That should do it."

First they had to drag the playhouse across the lawn and set it down next to the trampoline.

Bean noticed that the playhouse was not much taller than the trampoline. They were going to have to jump hard.

Next, Bean climbed up the plastic playhouse shutters until she was perched on the roof like a giant bird.

Ivy took a running jump at the playhouse and flung herself over the roof. "Oof," she said.

"You have to stand up," said Bean. "Or your jump will be too short."

"You go first," said Ivy in a muffled voice.

Bean rose slowly to her feet. The playhouse made a funny sound.

Ivy began to push herself up on her hands. There was another funny sound. It was a bending sort of sound. A crack-ing sort of sound.

The roof was caving in.

"Abandon ship!" Bean hollered and bounced onto the trampoline. But the two sides of the playhouse were folding around Ivy like a taco. She couldn't abandon ship. She couldn't do anything. Bean watched as Ivy sank closer and closer to the ground.

"Are you okay?" she asked.

"I'm fine," said Ivy.

After a few minutes, the playhouse stopped sinking, and Bean tried to pull Ivy out by yanking on her head. But Ivy said that hurt worse than being tacoed, so Bean yanked on the playhouse instead. Soon the roof de-caved enough for Ivy to squeeze out, and then Bean crawled inside and kicked the ceiling until the playhouse was almost the shape it had been before.

"Whew," said Bean, sitting down. "We're going to have to get some tape to fix that crack." She wiped her sweaty face with her sweaty hand. "Duct tape. I love fixing things."

"But Bean," said Ivy. "We didn't fix anything. We're still squids."

Dang. Bean had almost forgotten about that. Her duct-tape happiness faded. She was a squid. A friendly squid. "Maybe we'll get so sick we can't be in The World of Dance," she suggested.

"That's not a bad idea," said Ivy thoughtfully. "In fact, that's a great idea. We can't dance if we're sick. Let's get sick."

Sick. Well, it would hurt less than spraining her arm. "Okay, but how?" asked Bean.

"Germs," said Ivy. "We'll catch some germs and get sick."

"Germs," said Bean, thinking. "I know where germs are. At school. Ms. Aruba-Tate says the school is full of germs. That's why she's always making us wash our hands."

"But we don't want regular dirt germs. We want sick germs," said Ivy. "We'll have to find someone sick."

"Easy-peasy." Bean was definitely cheerful now. "Tomorrow we'll find the sickest person at school and touch him!"

GERMS OF HOPE

Ivy and Bean stood on the playground of Emerson School. Around them children were running and shouting. There were kids dangling from the monkey bars and dropping off the play structure. There were kids playing wall ball. There were kids arguing about four square. Some fifth-grade girls walked around the field, talking, which looked so incredibly boring that Bean hoped she would never get to fifth grade. Ivy and Bean leaned against the fence and watched. They were hunting for germs.

"I bet MacAdam is full of germs," whispered Bean.

MacAdam was eating dirt. He liked to do that. But other than eating dirt, he looked perfectly healthy.

"We need someone sicker," said Ivy. "Look for someone sitting down. If you sit down during recess, it's because you're sick."

They peered around the playground. "Drew is sitting down," said Bean, "but that's probably because the Yard Duty got him."

"What about that kid over there?" Ivy pointed to a first-grade-looking kid that Bean didn't know. He was sitting by himself on a bench.

"Hey! He coughed!" said Bean. "Let's get him!"

In a flash, they were at his side.

He looked up.

Ivy nudged Bean and pointed at his nose. It was runny.

"Are you sick?" asked Bean.

"Yes," said the kid. He coughed with his mouth wide open and then looked back up at them again. "What?"

"What have you got?" asked Ivy.

"What does it matter?" said Bean. "He's sick."

"I don't want to throw up," whispered Ivy.

"Oh," said Bean. She didn't want to throw up either. "You're not going to throw up, are you?" she asked the boy.

He looked a little worried. "I don't think so. Maybe."

Ivy took a step away. Bean stared at him, thinking about friendly squids. "Can I touch your face?" she asked finally. "Me and her, we need to get sick."

He wiped his nose. "Okay."

Bean stuck her hand on his face. It was kind of gross. "Breathe on me," she told him.

He puffed a big breath at her. She could feel the germs hitting her skin.

Ivy was standing far away in the bushes by now. "I'll just catch it from you," she called.

Bean rubbed her hands all over her face. "Thanks," she said to the kid. He sneezed.

Bean and Ivy knew about germs. They didn't make you sick right away. You had to wait at least a couple of hours. That was okay. Ivy and Bean didn't want to get sick during science. They liked science.

This month, science was Ocean Life. And today Ocean Life was fish prints. It was art and science mixed together, Ms. Aruba-Tate said. The second-graders nodded. They liked art, too.

Ms. Aruba-Tate explained about fish prints. You took a dead fish and painted it. Then you dropped it pretty hard on a piece of paper. When you picked it up again, there was a paint fish on your paper. Then you used your crayons to draw an undersea environment around the fish.

"Does everyone understand the instructions?" asked Ms. Aruba-Tate, looking around the classroom.

"Are the fish dead?" asked Zuzu.

"Yes, the fish are dead," said Ms. Aruba-Tate.

"Are you sure?"

"Completely sure," said Ms. Aruba-Tate. "Any other questions?"

The second-graders shook their heads. Fish prints sounded like fun.

"Now who is our supply person today?" asked Ms. Aruba-Tate.

"Eric!" shouted the second grade.

Eric leaped to his feet, waving his hands in the air. "Thank you, thank you!"

"Eric, please put one fish at each table," said Ms. Aruba-Tate, handing him a big plastic box.

Eric went around the room, carefully choosing the right dead fish for each table.

"Hurry up!" shouted everyone. Paint and dead fish. This was the best science yet.

Bean was itching to begin. When Eric reached her table, there were just two dead fish left in the box, but he couldn't decide between them. He looked at one and then the other. "Which one should I give you? The little one or the big one?"

"Just give us one!" shouted Bean.

"Maybe I should ask Ms. Aruba-Tate which one I should give you," Eric said.

Bean reached into his box and grabbed a dead fish.

"Ms. Aruba-Tate! Bean took a fish!"

Dang. Bean looked at her teacher. Was she going to be sent to the rug? Was she going to miss out on dead fish and paint?

But Ms. Aruba-Tate smiled at Bean. "Next time, don't grab, Bean."

Bean loved Ms. Aruba-Tate with all her heart.

Carefully Bean smeared her fish with green paint. She looked down and saw the fish's eye looking up. Poor fish. She decided to make the most beautiful fish print in the world, to make it up to the fish for being dead. Slowly she laid the fish on her paper and pressed. Then she pressed harder. It had to be good.

"Bean! Watch out!" squawked Vanessa.

Oops. She had pressed a little too hard.

The fish was kind of bent. She lifted it up and peeked at her print. That was kind of bent, too.

"You wrecked it!" said Vanessa. "And your fish print is all lumpy."

"It's not lumpy," said Bean.

"It's about to have babies," said Ivy.

"Yeah!" said Bean. She handed the fish to Ivy. "I did it on purpose," she said to Vanessa.

While Ivy made her fish print, Bean drew an undersea environment for her fish. Kelp. An octopus. A sea anemone. A wrecked ship with ghosts. Science was her favorite subject, for sure.

TIGHT TENTACLES

Ivy and Bean worked so hard on their fish prints that they forgot about getting sick. It was only on the way home that they remembered. Ivy looked down Bean's throat.

"It's pink," she said.

"It's always pink," said Bean. She felt her forehead. "I have a headache," she said.

"That's good," said Ivy encouragingly.

But when they got to Bean's house, Bean's mother said that a person with a headache was too sick to eat an ice-cream bar, and that's when Bean realized that she didn't have a headache after all. She felt fine.

She still felt fine the next day.

And the day after that.

Ivy touched a kid with a rash. Nothing. Eric sneezed on Bean eight times. Nothing. Half the kids in the first grade had lice, but Ivy and Bean decided that lice wouldn't help. Their mothers would make them be squids with lice.

By the end of the week, Ivy and Bean were completely unsick. They needed a new plan. But what?

AcHOo···
AcHOo···
AcHOo···
AcHOo···
AcHOo···
AcHOo···
AcHOo···
AcHOo···
AcHOo···

Usually Bean didn't worry much. In fact, grown-ups sometimes said she didn't worry enough. But that weekend, even while she was doing fun things like going to a fair that included a giant slide, Bean worried. Mostly it didn't feel like worry. What it felt like was fun with a little bit missing. When Bean came whooshing to the bottom of the giant slide, she thought, Why don't I feel totally great? And then she remembered. Because I have to be a squid in front of everyone.

Ivy worried, too. Ivy usually didn't worry about real life. Ivy usually worried about things like the Permian extinction, when a whole lot of animals died. The Permian extinction was very upsetting, but it had happened 250 million years ago, so it wasn't real life anymore.

This weekend Ivy didn't think about the Permian extinction. She thought about how she would feel being a squid on a stage in front of a whole lot of people. She knew how she would feel. Stupid. She would probably trip, because she usually did. And even if she didn't trip, she would be a squid. Everyone would know that Madame Joy had made her a squid because she was the worst dancer in the class. Too bad the Permian extinction didn't wipe out squids, Ivy thought.

On Sunday afternoon, Ivy went over to Bean's house to be measured for her squid costume. Bean's mother had said she would make both squid costumes because Ivy's mom didn't like to sew. But it wasn't even a real costume. Madame Joy's picture showed a white leotard with a circle of droopy white tentacles hanging from the waist.

Madame Joy said that tentacles were a breeze to make. Bean's mom didn't think so.

"Who ever heard of squid costumes, anyway?" she muttered.

"No complaining," said Bean.

"None of your lip there, missy," her mother said.

That was grown-ups for you. They never followed their own rules.

"I suppose I could stuff a bunch of tights and sew them on," Bean's mother mumbled. Bean and Ivy exchanged looks.

"Tights?" Bean said. "Like the kind you wear on your legs?"

Her mother looked up. "Yes, tights. Stuffed tights. For the tentacles. Do you have a better idea?"

Bean thought of the Wilis in their long feathery dresses. She thought of herself with stuffed tights bouncing around her waist.

"Tights it is!" said her mother.

"We're going to look like idiots," said Bean.

"No complaining," said her mother.

+ + + + + +

Monday started out badly. Ms. Aruba-Tate was at choking class. The Principal had told her to take choking class so she would know what to do if a student choked. Bean said if someone choked, you dangled them upside down by their ankles until whatever it was fell out. Ms. Aruba-Tate said she didn't think so, but she would find out.

Ms. Aruba-Tate's substitute was Teacher Star. Teacher Star wasn't mean, but she never stopped singing. She sat on Ms. Aruba-Tate's stool and strummed her guitar and sang. She told the second-graders to sing along, but they didn't want to, so she sang alone.

She sang and sang and sang some more.

Ivy read her book under her desk. Bean thought about choking. Then she thought about ballet class. She thought about Dulcie and her pink chiffon dance skirt. She thought about white tentacles made out of stuffed tights.

"There's a little blue planet in the sky," sang Teacher Star.

+ + + + + +

It was nice to see Ms. Aruba-Tate again after lunch recess, but by then Bean was too busy thinking about ballet class to pay attention to what Ms. Aruba-Tate was saying. Something about permission slips. She was waving a piece of paper. Who knew what it was about?

"Does anyone have any questions about our trip?" asked Ms. Aruba-Tate.

"What trip?" asked Bean.

"Will someone tell Bean about our field trip to the aquarium?" said Ms. Aruba-Tate. "Emma?"

"We're going on a field trip to the aquarium," said Emma.

"To see some ocean life," said Dusit.

"We're going to see them feed the sharks," said Eric. "Raw meat."

"And baby penguins," said Zuzu.

"They're going to feed the baby penguins to the sharks," said Eric. He clashed his teeth together, being a shark.

"Eric," said Ms. Aruba-Tate.

"Just kidding, Ms. Aruba-Tate," said Eric.

"Oh!" said Ivy in a very loud voice. Everyone looked at her. Ivy hardly ever said anything in a very loud voice.

"Ivy?" asked Ms. Aruba-Tate.

Ivy gave Bean an enormous smile. Then she turned to Ms. Aruba-Tate and said, "I was just thinking about how much I love ocean life."

BYE-BYE, BALLET

"We're saved!" hissed Ivy, pulling Bean toward the door.

"Saved from what?" Bean hissed back.

"Being squids!" squealed Ivy. She raced out into the breezeway. Bean's sleeve was in her hand, so Bean raced with her. Together they left the school behind and hurried toward Pancake Court.

"Okay," puffed Bean, "how are we saved?"

Ivy stopped. "The field trip! We're going to run away! We'll run away to the aquarium, and we'll stay there until after The World of Dance is over!"

Running away! What a great idea! Bean had been waiting for years to run away. What she had been waiting for was a reason. She didn't want to hurt her parents' feelings by running away for no reason. The World of Dance was a great reason. This was the chance of a lifetime.

Oh yeah. Bean suddenly remembered the other reason she had never run away. "What about food?" she asked.

"Easy-peasy-Parcheesi," said Ivy. "I read about it in a book. You know how people throw money in fountains? We scrape it off the bottom of the fountain after the aquarium is closed at night, and then we buy food with it."

That was pretty smart. Bean was impressed. Also, it would be fun to walk in a fountain without grown-ups freaking out about it. "Cool," she said. "Where will we sleep?"

"We'll find a good spot once we get there. Aquariums are good for sleeping because they're dark."

"And quiet. Fish are very quiet." Bean pictured herself drifting off to sleep with fish swirling around her. It would be nice. "It'll be like sleeping on a boat."

Ivy rubbed her hands together. "In this book I read, the kids filled their clarinet cases with extra underwear, but we'll use our backpacks."

"My backpack is pretty big."

"We should bring jackets, too. And money. In the book, they brought all their money."

"Why do we need money if we're going to scrape it out of the fountain?" asked Bean. "Besides, I only have four dollars and some coins."

"I've got twenty-six and some coins," said Ivy. "But I don't want to spend it. I'm saving for a glass doll."

"There will be plenty of money in the fountain," Bean decided.

"And we'll get clean at the same time," said Ivy.

"Boy," Bean said, shaking her head. "It's too bad I wasted all that time worrying."

+ + + + + +

Somehow, knowing that they were going to run away made ballet class better. "Still not good," said Bean. "But better."

"I don't know," said Ivy. She was watching Dulcie do an arabesque. An arabesque was when you stretched out one arm and one leg at the same time.

Arabesques made Ivy fall over. Dulcie could arabesque all day long. "Bet she puts glue on her shoes," muttered Ivy.

"Very nice, Dulcie," said Madame Joy.

"Thank you, Madame Jwah!" said Dulcie.

Now instead of being butterflies at the end of ballet class, they practiced "Wedding Beneath the Sea." Dulcie swayed and kitty-jumped and fluttered her fingers. Two starfish girls twirled with their arms out. Two sea-horse girls galloped in and out of the starfish. Two tuna girls glided together across the floor. Ivy and Bean, the friendly squids, stayed in one place and waved their arms.

"Call this dancing?" Bean whispered. "This is standing."

"Enter the prince!" cried Madame Joy.

The prince was a girl wearing a black leotard and a red hat that looked like a tiny pillowcase. The prince was the second-crummiest part in "Wedding Beneath the Sea," but it was way better than being a friendly squid. The prince at least got to leap. The prince-girl leaped toward Dulcie while Dulcie fluttered away. Then the prince got down on one knee and waved her arms at Dulcie. Then Dulcie nodded, and all the other fishy things got in a circle and danced around them. Except the two friendly squids. Madame Joy said they were like doormen. They guarded the entrance to the mermaid palace.

Finally Madame Joy clapped her hands. Class was over. For Ivy and Bean, it was especially over. Next week they'd be living at the aquarium.

Ivy grinned at Bean. "Bye-bye, ballet," she whispered.

"Down with squids!" Bean whispered back.

The night before the field trip Bean filled her backpack with useful items. Band-Aids? Check. Pencil? Check. String? Check. Underwear? Check. Bag of salt? Check. Nancy had told her once that all you needed to stay alive was salt and water. Bean figured there would be plenty of water at the aquarium.

Bean zipped her backpack closed. She looked around her room. It seemed like she should be discussing important things with Ivy. She couldn't think of any important things, but she called Ivy anyway.

"Are you ready?" she asked.

"Who's this?" said Ivy.

"Bean!"

"Oh. Hi, Bean," said Ivy. She didn't like talking on the phone. "What do you want?"

"Are you ready? Say ten-four if you are."

"Say what?" asked Ivy.

"Ten-four," said Bean.

"Fourteen," said Ivy.

"No! It means yes," said Bean.

"Yes what?"

"Ivy! Yes, I'm ready!" yelled Bean.

"Oh. I'm ready, too. Good-bye." Ivy hung up.

Forget it. Bean went back to her room. It was almost bedtime, which meant it was almost morning, which meant it was almost running-away time. Bean could hardly wait.

VERY FISHY

Ms. Aruba-Tate's class swarmed off the bus. They were proud. Their bus behavior had been excellent, if you didn't count Marga-Lee and Dusit.

They stampeded up the stairs toward the aquarium's front door. Who would get there first? Who would be the best?

"Boys and girls! Stop!" hollered Ms. Aruba-Tate. They stopped. Ms. Aruba-Tate didn't holler very often. "Boys and girls! Stay where you are! Don't move! Stay with your buddy! Try to stay together!"

The white marble patio outside the aquarium was full of hollering teachers and wandering kids. There were kids sliding down the handrail on the stairs. There were boys throwing their backpacks at each other. There were girls walking along the rim of the fountain. All the teachers were trying to get all the kids to stand still. What a nuthouse, thought Bean.

"Boys and girls! Follow me!" shouted Ms. Aruba-Tate. "Stay with your buddy!"

Linking arms, Ivy and Bean climbed the stairs toward the big golden doors.

"Our new home," Bean whispered.

They went inside. The aquarium was big and dim, with dark hallways like arms leading off in many directions. It was sort of greenish all over, and even with hundreds of kids wandering around, it was quiet.

"Okay," said Ivy, pulling out a list. "The first thing we do is find a good hiding place."

But they couldn't find a good hiding place because Ms. Aruba-Tate was calling them over to the alligator pit. The second-graders clustered around the pit and stared down at the alligators.

"Look!" Bean nudged Ivy. "There's money in there!" Bright coins sparkled in the slimy alligator water.

Ivy looked. "No way am I going in an alligator pit to get money," she said.

"Oh. Right." Bean stared at the money. What a waste. The alligators seemed dead anyway. They didn't even move. Maybe she could just slip in and out.

One of the alligators spread its mouth wide in a yawn.

Maybe not.

"Stay together!" called Ms. Aruba-Tate, leading them from the alligator pit to a dark hallway. "Now we will see Coastal Zones."

Ivy nodded at Bean. Coastal Zones sounded like a good place to make a getaway.

"When do we eat lunch?" yelled Paul. "I'm starving to death."

"Now," whispered Ivy. She and Bean started to walk backward.

"There will be no eating inside the aquarium," said Ms. Aruba-Tate. "Ivy! Bean! Stay with the group!"

"Boy, does she have sharp eyes," Bean muttered.

Coastal Zones turned out to be tide pools. Tide pools were good because you got to stick your hands in them. Ivy and Bean decided to run away later. Ivy held an orange starfish, which was really called a sea star and had eyes at the ends of its arms. Pretty neat.

A sea anemone wrapped its soft tentacles around Bean's finger. She

hoped it didn't hurt when she pulled her finger
away.

After Coastal Zones, there were penguins.
Bean and Ivy liked penguins, but Zuzu loved
them. She cried when it was time to go. Eric
said he was going to freak if they didn't get to
sharks soon, so Ms. Aruba-Tate let them skip
shrimp and move straight to sharks.

"I want to see sharks," said Bean. "Then
we'll go."

Ivy nodded. She wanted to see sharks, too.

As it turned out, sharks were not that exciting. For one, they were small. And they swam around in circles, zip, zip. They didn't care if the second grade wanted to see them or not. They just zipped around.

"Come along, boys and girls," called Ms. Aruba-Tate. "Let's investigate the Kelp Forest."

The Kelp Forest. Boringsville. Bean nodded to Ivy. Ivy nodded to Bean. They waited beside the shark glass while the rest of the class surged forward. Ms. Aruba-Tate was listening to Emma tell about the time she was seasick. She didn't notice Ivy and Bean.

No one noticed.

In a minute, they were all alone with the sharks.

Now that Ms. Aruba-Tate's class was gone, Bean and Ivy could hear the sharks. They could hear them move through the water.

"Come on." Ivy pulled on Bean's sleeve.

"Wait a second." Bean leaned close to the glass wall. Bean wondered if they could hear her. "Hi," she said. The sharks swam around, their black eyes empty. They didn't care. "Let's get out of here," she said to Ivy.

They turned and scurried down a hall lined with little tanks of fish.

When they got to the end of that hall, they turned down another.

And then another. They had done it.

They were runaways.

OCEAN LIFE GONE BAD

Ivy and Bean came to a gray room. It didn't have any ocean life in it. What it did have in it were a lot of dishes.

"We must be near the cafeteria," said Ivy.

A man walked into the room pushing a cart. He didn't look surprised to see them, but he didn't look happy either. "No kids in here," he said. "Cafeteria's that way." He pointed to a door.

"Okay," said Bean. She and Ivy went through a different door.

Now they were in a dark hallway. A dark, small hallway. They could just barely see the sign on the wall. It said, "Life without Light: Creatures of the Deep Sea."

"Perfect!" said Ivy.

"Perfect? For what?" asked Bean. It didn't look perfect to her. It looked dark.

"Life without Light." said Ivy. "It's great for sleeping. Plus, no one will be able to see us."

Bean looked around the little hall. "We're going to sleep in here?"

"No. This is just where they put the sign. The fish and stuff are in there." She pointed to a doorway.

Together they walked into a long, narrow room. At least Bean thought it was a long, narrow room. She couldn't really tell because it was so dark. It was even darker than the hall.

"Why don't they turn on some lights?" whispered Bean. It seemed like a whispering place.

"It's showing what it's like in the deep sea. The sun doesn't get all the way down there," whispered Ivy.

"So that's all? Just a dark room?" Bean shook her head.

"I don't know. I can't tell. Do you see fish tanks anywhere?"

Bean looked hard into the darkness. She could see some glimmering on the wall. Maybe it was glass. Or something else. Bean started to get a worried feeling. "Why aren't there any people in here?" she asked.

"I don't know," Ivy said again. Bean could see the outline of Ivy's head as she looked from side to side. "Maybe the sign was old. Maybe there's nothing in here."

For a moment, they stood there in the dark. It was so quiet that they heard the sound of the quiet. Bean began to think of all the things that might be slithering silently toward them.

"Ivy? I'm not liking this so much," she said.

Ivy linked her arm into Bean's. That was better. A little. "There's got to be a light switch in here somewhere," said Ivy. "If we walk around, I bet we'll find one. And once we turn on the light, we'll figure out where to hide our backpacks."

Slowly, with their arms out, they walked toward the wall. Bean's hands brushed against cool glass. No light switches there. She felt around its edges.

"Hey," said Ivy. "Here's a button thing. Should I push it?"

"Um," said Bean. "What if it opens a trapdoor and water gushes out?"

Too late. Ivy had pushed the button. The wall in front of them began to glow with red light. For a second, they blinked at the brightness. And then they saw. Behind the glass was black water rising high above their heads. They pressed their faces to the window. Was it just empty water?

"I don't see any fish," Bean began to say—and then a massive mouth came hurtling toward them, shining with thousands of needle teeth. "YIKES!" Bean took an enormous leap backward, dragging Ivy behind her.

"Holy moly cannoli!" she squeaked. "What the heck is that?"

Ivy didn't say anything, but her hand held tight to Bean's. The giant mouth was attached to a long snaky creature that glared at them with tiny bright eyes.

"I guess this is what it's like at the bottom of the sea," whispered Ivy.

Bean shivered.

On the other side of the glass wall, a fish swam by, a thin arm sprouting from its head. At the end of the arm was a glowing lump. The fish swished its head from side to side, and the glowing lump swung like a lantern.

Slowly the two girls made their way around the room. Long white worms poked from tubes. See-through fish wiggled along, trailing other fish with glowing eyeballs. Shining blobs with no heads or tails rolled on the floor of the tank. Were they alive?

"Could we turn the lights off again?" Ivy asked in a small voice. "I can't stop looking at those blobs."

Bean reached over to the button under the glass and pressed it. The red light faded into

darkness. Thick nighttime darkness. With worms and giant mouths in it.

"Ivy?" said Bean. "I don't think I can live in here for two weeks."

"Sure you can," said Ivy, but her voice didn't sound sure. "They're inside tanks. Tank glass is super-strong."

There was a pause.

"I keep thinking they're watching us," said Bean.

"I keep thinking the glass is going to break," said Ivy.

Bean pictured the giant mouth whizzing toward her. She jumped up and pressed the button again.

But it was a different button. The red light did not begin to glow. Instead, a serious voice began to talk.

"The most famous creature of the deep sea can't be seen in an aquarium because it has never been captured alive. The giant squid, which may reach a length of forty feet, is shown here in a rare video. . . ."

The voice went on talking, but Bean and Ivy didn't hear it.

They were watching the video. An enormous white blob flapped in empty black water, its long, blubbery white arms trailing behind. Around and around it spun and ruffled and circled, dancing in the water. It was like a horrible Wili, Bean thought. Its legs flailed and waved. Then, with a giant flap and whirl, the squid shot toward them. Its head, huge and soft, turned, and suddenly a single monster eye, an eye the size of a plate, stared right into theirs. It could see them.

For a second, Ivy and Bean stood frozen.

And then they began to run.

IN HOT WATER

Bean couldn't stop running. She was gasping for air and her backpack was slamming into her shoulders, but she couldn't stop running.

Ivy slammed into a kid. "Excuse me," she gasped.

"Watch out!" yelled a teacher as they pounded by. "No running in the aquarium!"

They couldn't stop. The squid was back there, waiting for them. They had to get out.

They tore up a dark hallway filled with sardines and down a dark hallway filled with jellyfish.

They flashed past the sharks, past the penguins, past the alligator pit, and exploded through the heavy golden doors into the outside world.

Air instead of water. Light instead of darkness. People instead of fish.

They were safe.

For a moment, they stood there, panting and gasping. I love light, thought Bean. I love air. I love this white marble patio—

"BEAN! IVY! WHERE ON EARTH HAVE YOU BEEN?" Ms. Aruba-Tate rushed toward them with her arms open. "Did you get lost? We were looking everywhere! Oh dear, I was so worried!" She gathered them up in a giant hug. "Oh dear," she said, "oh, honeys!"

Ivy and Bean let themselves be hugged. It felt nice, after that squid, to be hugged.

"We're okay," said Bean.

"We got lost," Ivy said quickly. That was kind of true.

"Oh, sweeties!" Ms. Aruba-Tate hugged them again. "Why didn't you go to one of the guards? Didn't I tell you to go to a guard if you got lost?"

"There weren't any guards," said Bean. That was completely true.

Now the rest of Ms. Aruba-Tate's class was clustering around.

"There you are!" said Emma. "See, Ms. Aruba-Tate, I told you they weren't dead."

"We got to see the eels and you didn't," said Eric. "They're hecka gross."

"I can't believe you got lost," said Vanessa. "Where'd you go?"

"Into a part of the aquarium that no one has ever seen before," said Ivy.

"There was this squid with eyes this big," said Bean, holding her hands apart.

"You're making that up," said Vanessa.

"We're not!" said Ivy. "There were white worms and this mouth with teeth—"

"Girls!" interrupted Ms. Aruba-Tate. She looked very serious. "Girls, are you telling me that you were wandering around the aquarium having a good time? That you didn't even try to find us?"

Ivy and Bean looked at each other. "Um," said Bean.

"We were trying to find you, Ms. Aruba-Tate," said Ivy. "We just happened to see a few worms and things while we were trying."

"Ivy and Bean, I am very disappointed in you," Ms. Aruba-Tate began. "Our class has discussed safety rules many times, and I was counting on you being mature enough to understand that a field trip is an educational experience, not an excuse for bad behavior."

All the way to the bus Ms. Aruba-Tate talked about disappointment and safety and bad behavior. Ivy and Bean nodded. They said she was right and they were wrong. They said they were sorry.

She was going to have to tell their parents, Ms. Aruba-Tate said.

Ivy and Bean nodded. They knew she had to.

They also knew that their parents were going to be mad. And that they were going to get in trouble.

But Ivy and Bean didn't care as long as each of them could hold one of Ms. Aruba-Tate's hands on the bus ride home. As long as they never had to go back to that aquarium and see that squid again in their whole lives.

SQUIDARINAS

They were right. Bean's mother was mad. "This is not what I expect from you, Bernice Blue. When you go on a trip of any kind, I expect you to listen to the grown-up in charge. This is something we've discussed a thousand times." Bean's mother folded her arms and glared at Bean.

Bean could tell she was supposed to say something. "I'm sorry," she said.

"I should think so!" said her mother. She glared some more. "Well! We'll talk about the consequences this evening when Daddy comes home. In the meantime, both of you go upstairs and try on your ballet costumes. And I don't want to hear any complaining!"

Bean and Ivy walked quietly upstairs. Quietly they closed the door to Bean's room. "Whew," said Ivy. "That was a close one."

"It's not over yet," said Bean. "Your mom still has to get mad."

"I know," said Ivy. "But at least none of them found out about the running-away part."

"We've got to get rid of the evidence," said Bean, busily pulling the bag of salt, the Band-Aids, the string, and the underwear out of her backpack. She stuffed it all under her bed.

Ivy did the same.

"Jeez!" Bean slumped against her bed. "What a day."

Ivy lay down on the floor. "I'm pooped."

"Are you trying on those costumes?" shouted Bean's mother from downstairs.

"Sheesh," said Bean, getting up. "Work, work, work. That's all I do." The white leotards lay across her bed, stuffed tights legs tangled around them. "Come on," said Bean. "You have to try yours on, too." Ivy sighed and got up. Together they untangled the tights legs and got undressed and pulled on the white leotards. Bean looked at Ivy in her white leotard with ten white legs dangling from her waist.

Ivy looked at Bean. "I don't think Madame Joy has ever seen a real squid," she said.

Bean thought about the long, blubbery white legs. It made her head prickle. "Remember its legs?"

Ivy nodded. "And its eye? Remember how it looked at us?"

"Like it was excited. Like it could hardly wait to squeeze the life out of us," said Bean.

"Like we were food," agreed Ivy.

"Squids are *not* friendly," Bean announced.

Ivy lifted up one of her white tights legs and

shook it. "A real squid would wrap its legs around Dulcie and squish her."

Bean giggled. "And then it would eat the starfish and the sea horses." She bonked Ivy with one of her tights legs. "And the prince."

Ivy bonked her back. "And then it would look at the audience with its humongo eye and say, 'And you people are my dessert.'"

There was a pause.

"You know," Bean said thoughtfully, "we could use your face paint to make big black eyes."

There was another pause. Ivy and Bean looked at each other.

"Madame Joy will kill us," said Ivy.

"We won't do anything," said Bean. "We'll just look more like real squids. She won't mind."

"In a way, she should be glad," said Ivy. "We'll be teaching everyone what squids are really like."

"Yeah, it's educational," said Bean. For the first time, she felt a little bit excited about being a squid. "And maybe, at the very end, after the rest of the dance is over, we can be two squid trying to squeeze the life out of each other."

"Yeah!" said Ivy cheerfully. "Like this!"

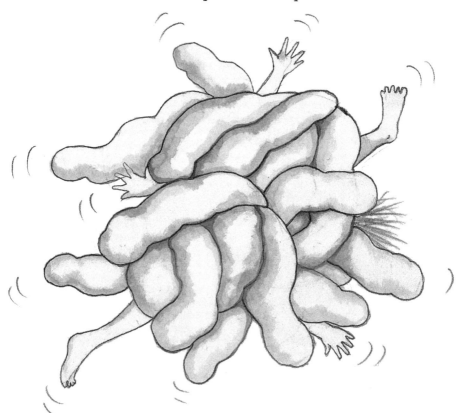

She jumped at Bean and wrapped three of her tentacles around Bean's arm.

Bean hit Ivy over the head with a tights leg and growled. The two unfriendly squids bashed and squeezed each other until they had to lie down on the floor.

"You know what?" said Bean after a minute.

"What?" said Ivy.

"By the time we get through with it, 'Wedding Beneath the Sea' is going to be a lot like *Giselle*. Only more exciting."

Ivy smiled. "Plus more scientific."

"I just knew we'd end up liking ballet!" said Bean happily.

ivy + BEAN

BOOK 7

SNEAK PREVIEW OF THE NEXT
IVY & BEAN ADVENTURE

There had been a problem in Bean's house. The problem was staples. Bean loved staples. She loved them so much that she had stapled things that weren't supposed to be stapled. The things looked better stapled, but her mother didn't think so, and now Bean was outside.

She was going to be outside for a long time.

She looked at her back yard. Same old yard, same old trampoline, same old dinky plastic playhouse, same old pile of buckets and ropes and stilts. None of them was any fun. Maybe she could play junkyard crash. Junkyard crash was when you stacked up all the stuff you could find and then drove the toy car into the stack. But it was no fun alone. Bean got up and scuffed across the nice green lawn until she reached the not-so-nice green lawn. This part of Bean's lawn had holes and lumps in it. The lumps were mostly places where Bean had buried treasure for kids of the future.

Bean picked up a shovel. To heck with kids of the future. She was bored now. And maybe a kind old guy had seen her digging and added something interesting to her treasure, like a ruby skull or a dinosaur egg.

Bean didn't bury her treasure very deep, so it was easy to dig up. This treasure was inside a paper bag, but the paper bag wasn't doing so well. It wasn't really a paper bag anymore. "Oh my gosh!" said Bean loudly. "I've found treasure!" She pulled apart the clumps of paper. What a disappointment. No ruby skull. No dinosaur egg. Just the same stuff she had buried two weeks ago: dental floss, tweezers, and a magnifying glass. Some treasure.

Bean flopped over on her stomach. "I'm dying of boredom," she moaned, hoping her mother would hear. "I'm dyyy-ing." She coughed in a dying sort of way—"Huh-ACK!"—and then lay still. Anyone looking from the porch would think she was dead. And then that person would feel bad.

Bean lay very still.

Still.

She could hear her heart thumping.

She could feel the hairs on her arm moving.

Bean opened her eyes. There was an ant scurrying over her arm. Bean pulled the magnifying glass over and peered at the ant.

Her arm was like a mountain, and the little ant was like a mountain climber, stumbling along with a tired expression on his face. Poor hardworking ant. She watched as he dodged between hairs and charged down the other side of her arm toward the ground. She offered him a blade of grass to use as a slide, but that seemed to confuse him. He paused, looked anxiously right and left, and then continued down her arm. He had a plan and he was going to stick to it. Bean watched through the magnifying glass as he scuttled into the grass, rushing along the ground between blades. He was late. He was in trouble. He met another ant by banging into him, but they didn't even stop to talk. They rushed away in opposite directions.

Bean followed her ant to a patch of dry dirt. There he plunged down a hole.

"Come back," whispered Bean. She liked her ant. Maybe he would come out if she poked his house. She found a thin stick and touched the top of the hole. Four ants streamed out and raced in four different directions. Bean didn't think any of them was her ant.

Bean watched the ant hole for a long time. Ants came and went. They all seemed to know where they were going. They all seemed to have important jobs. None of them seemed to notice that they were puny little nothings compared to Bean.

Bean dragged the hose toward the ant hole. She didn't turn the hose on. That would be mean. But she let a little bit of water dribble into the hole, and watched as the dirt erupted with ants. Thousands of ants flung themselves this way and that, racing to safety.

"Help, help," whispered Bean. "Flood!"

The ants ran in orderly lines away from the water. Some were holding little grains above their heads. They were the hero ants. But even the non-hero ants were busy. They were all far too busy to notice Bean watching them through the magnifying glass. To them, she was like a planet. She wasn't part of their world. She was too big and too far away for them to see.

Bean looked up into the sky. What if someone was watching her through a giant magnifying glass and thinking the same thing she was? What if she was as small as an ant compared to that someone? And what if that someone was an ant compared to the next world after that?

Wow.

Bean waved at the sky. Hi, out there, she thought.